For Jasmine

First published in the UK in 2004 by
Red Kite Books, an imprint of Haldane Mason Ltd
PO Box 34196, London NW10 3YB
email: info@haldanemason.com

ISBN 1-902463-54-4

A HALDANE MASON BOOK

Colour reproduction by One Thirteen Ltd, UK
Printed in the UAE

Medical consultant: **Dr Rob Hicks**

Please note:
The information presented in this book is intended as a support to
professional advice and care. It is not a substitute for medical diagnosis or
treatment. Always notify and consult your doctor if your child is ill.

"The voice of dyslexic people"

The British Dyslexia Association
Reg. Charity no. 289243

Brian has Dyslexia

Jenny Leigh

Illustrated by Woody Fox

ReD KiTE

Name: Brian Bear

Age: 7

Sex: Boy

Case Notes: Brian Bear's mother thought he was doing badly at school because he couldn't see the blackboard, but Brian's eyes were fine – there was another reason why he found reading and writing so hard.

Doctor R Spot

Brian had spent the day with his friend Humphrey. Humphrey's dad had cooked a yummy Sunday lunch, and the two friends had spent the afternoon riding their bikes along the track by the river. Brian was a bit wobbly on his bike. He just couldn't seem to balance, steer and pedal all at the same time. Humphrey was a really good bike rider and he raced ahead.

"Wait for me!" called Brian.

On his way home, Brian suddenly found a car driving straight towards him on the same side of the road! *Beep-beep!* The car swerved around Brian and screeched to a halt. Brian wobbled like mad and just managed to stop without falling off.

Mr Antelope jumped out of the car. "What do you think you're doing on the wrong side of the road?" he shouted. He was very cross!

"Sorry, Mr Antelope," said Brian. "I didn't think I *was* on the wrong side."

"Well, you should know your left from your right at your age, Brian!" snapped Mr Antelope angrily, and he drove off in his car, a bit too fast!

Mrs Bear was angry with Brian, too. "I had Mr Antelope on the 'phone for half an hour," she said. "Really, Brian, if I can't trust you to ride your bike safely, I won't let you ride it at all."

"Oh M-u-u-u-m!" wailed Brian. He loved his bike, and he was sure that Humphrey would find someone else to play with if he didn't have one.

"Lights out now," said Mrs Bear firmly. "You need to be up early for school tomorrow."

"School!" thought Brian as he lay in the dark, and he let out a big sigh. He found school work very hard.

The next morning, Mrs Bear couldn't get Brian out of bed. "My head hurts so much, I just want to lie still," he whispered.

"All right, dear," said Mrs Bear worriedly, "but I'm going to take you to see Doctor Spot, because this is the fourth bad headache you've had this term."

Later that day, Brian and Mrs Bear were in Doctor Spot's surgery, telling him all about Brian's headaches.

"Could his eyes be the problem?" asked Mrs Bear. "He does have a lot of trouble with his reading and writing — maybe he can't see the letters or numbers on the blackboard."

"Yes, it is a good idea to have his eyes tested," said Doctor Spot. "What's your favourite class at school, Brian?"

"I love art," said Brian, "and I love making up stories — as long as I don't have to write them down, or read them out."

"What happens when you do that?" asked Doctor Spot.

"Well, I get all in a muddle and they don't come out right," said Brian, sadly.

"Hmmm," said Doctor Spot and he turned to Mrs Bear. "I think it would be a good idea for you and Mr Bear to go and talk to Brian's teacher about this." Mrs Bear wasn't sure how the teacher could help Brian's headaches, but she said she would talk to the teacher anyway.

Mr and Mrs Bear went to the school for a meeting with Brian's teacher.

"I'm so glad you've come to see me," said Mrs Flamingo. "As I said in my letter, I am worried about Brian's progress at school."

"What letter?" asked Mr Bear.

"Why, I sent a letter home with Brian last week!" said Mrs Flamingo. "Brian is a very bright little bear," she went on. "He works very hard, but he finds reading and writing difficult. I would like him to meet someone who could tell us if Brian has a special learning problem."

"Oh, dear!" said Mrs Bear. "Is that what gives him his headaches?"

"Well, in a way it might be," said Mrs Flamingo.

Brian went to see Mr Parrot, who was a specialist teacher. Mr Parrot explained that they were going to do some tests to see if they could work out why Brian was finding some of his schoolwork so hard.

"Oh!" said Brian. "I'm not very good at tests."

"Why do you think that is, Brian?" asked Mr Parrot.

"My friend Mike says it's because I'm stupid," said Brian, glumly.

"Well, he doesn't sound like a very good friend," said Mr Parrot. "Besides, Miss Flamingo tells me you are very clever, and you won a prize in painting last week."

"Yes," said Brian slowly, "but everyone laughed at me because I had to write my name on the painting and it came out all wrong!" His eyes filled with tears.

"No, I can't," said Mr Parrot, "but there are things we can do to help you."

Mr Parrot gave Brian lots of tests to do to see if he was right about Brian's dyslexia. There were letter and word tests, numbers and spelling, reading and writing, listening and memory. Then Mr Parrot asked Brian to look at a picture and make up a story about what was happening in it. By the time his parents came to collect him, poor Brian was quite worn out!

"Oh, dear!" said Mrs Bear when Mr Parrot told them that Brian did have dyslexia. "What do we do now?"

"There's lots you can do to help Brian, and lots that he can do to help himself," said Mr Parrot. "And I would like to see him once a week for some special teaching."

23

The next day, Mr Bear went out and bought a lovely set of wooden letters in bright colours. Each day, he and Brian did a little bit of work with them. At first Brian had to find the letter his father asked for. Then they both said the name of the letter out loud and the sound it made. Finally Mr Bear covered up the letter and Brian had to write it. Sometimes he got it wrong and he was really cross with himself, but after a while he started to get more of them right.

Mrs Bear made some letter cards. Then she asked Brian to paint something on the other side of the card that started with that letter. He painted a hat on the back of the 'h' card, and a sun on the back of the 's', and he painted himself on the 'b' card! " 'B' can be for Brian or bear," he said, proudly. "This is fun, Mum!"

Humphrey and Brian rode their bikes along the track by the river.

"Why did your Mum let you have your bike back?" called Humphrey over his shoulder. "Have you learned your left from your right?"

"Not really," said Brian. "I still mix them up sometimes, but Mum decided that left and right don't matter so much — it is more important to know the wrong side of the road from the right side."

"So how do you know that?" asked Humphrey.

"Easy!" cried Brian. "Mum put a bell on my handlebar, and as long I ride with it on the same side as the edge of the road, I know I'm on my side!"

Brring brring! Brian rang his bell, and the two friends cycled off together.

27

"Dad! Mum!" shouted Brian as he arrived home from school. "Guess what? My team won the end-of-term quiz today!"

"Fantastic!" said his father, and he gave Brian a great big bear hug. "Did you get a prize?" Brian held up a large bag of sweets.

Brian smiled all through supper, and he smiled when he was in the bath. He was still smiling when Mrs Bear tucked him into bed.

"Who would have thought that a quiz would make you so happy?" she chuckled.

"It's because I'm not stupid after all, Mum," said Brian happily. "I've just got dyslexia!" And he fell fast asleep — smiling!

Parents' pages: Dyslexia

What are the indicators?

There are many indicators for dyslexia. If your child displays some of the behaviours listed below, it does not necessarily mean that they have dyslexia. If your child displays a cluster of the behaviours and does not progress, discuss your concerns with their school.

Pre-School
- Late speech development
- Persistent jumbled phrases
- Difficulty learning nursery rhymes
- Difficulty in dressing
- Likes being read to but shows no interest in letters or words
- Poor attention span
- Excessive tripping, bumping into things, and falling over
- Difficulty with catching, throwing, or kicking a ball
- Forgets names, colours, etc.
- Difficulty keeping a simple rhythm

Primary School
- Difficulty with reading and spelling
- Puts letters and figures the wrong way round (mirror writing)
- Leaves letters out of words or puts them in the wrong order
- Difficulty remembering tables, alphabet, formulas, etc.
- Sometimes confuses 'b' and 'd' and words such as 'no' and 'on'
- Still uses fingers or marks on paper to do simple sums
- Takes longer than average to do written work
- Difficulty with tying laces, tie, dressing
- Still confuses left and right
- Confuses days of the week, months of the year

What should I do?

If you are concerned about your child's development, discuss it with their teacher. The school will be able to advise you on appropriate assessment, and if necessary, specialist teaching help. If your child is dyslexic, it is important that you build good relationships with their teachers throughout their schooling. If the school is uncooperative, you may need to seek independent assessment and help. Have your child's eyesight and hearing checked to ensure these are not contributing to their difficulties.

Will my child always be dyslexic?

Much can be done to help dyslexic children, but dyslexia cannot be 'cured'. Dyslexic children are often labelled as 'stupid' or 'disruptive' and it is important that the condition is recognized as early as possible, and specialist help is sought. With the right support, many of the difficulties caused by dyslexia can be overcome.

Doctor Spot says:

- If you have a partner, make sure you are both involved in consultations with the school or any specialists
- Some dyslexic children work extremely hard to keep up at school. Don't pressure them to do extra reading and writing at home if they are tired
- When teaching children to do up buttons, always get them to start from the bottom where it is easier for them to see what they are doing
- Watch television with your child and discuss what you have seen
- Many dyslexic children have areas of high ability as well as learning difficulties. Encourage their strengths and praise them when they do well
- When teaching your child to tie shoelaces or a tie, stand behind them if you are both right or left-handed, but in front if you are opposite-handed. Get your child to describe each action
- Treat aggression and anti-social behaviour gently but firmly. Remember that all children behave like this sometimes – don't blame it all on their dyslexia!
- Don't let your child use dyslexia as an excuse, either. Reassure them that some things may take longer, but that they will get there in the end
- Your child may be teased at school by classmates. Watch out for stress signs such as bedwetting or introversion. Encourage your child to talk about their emotions
- A dyslexic child may take up a lot of time, but try to make sure this is not at the expense of other children in the family

For more information on dyslexia, contact the British Dyslexia Association at www.bda-dyslexia.org.uk (helpline: 0118 966 8271; email: info@dyslexiahelp-bda.demon.co.uk)

Titles in the Doctor Spot series:

Brian has Dyslexia ISBN: 1-902463-54-4
Brian is a very bright bear, but keeps getting his words muddled up. Dr Spot helps him to understand his problem.

Charlie has Asthma ISBN: 1-902463-68-4
Charlie the Cheetah is always running out of breath. Doctor Spot tells him what's wrong and gives Charlie a special inhaler.

Emma has Measles ISBN: 1-902463-44-7
When Emma the Elephant catches measles, it looks as though she's going to miss her star part in the play.

George has Meningitis ISBN: 1-902463-91-9
George the Gorilla is feeling very ill. His sister, Gloria, learned about the tell-tale signs of meningitis at school, and gets her father to call in Doctor Spot without delay.

Harriet has Tonsillitis ISBN: 1-902463-37-4
Harriet the Hippopotamus has a nasty case of tonsillitis. Doctor Spot is at hand to make her feel better.

Lawrence has Nits ISBN: 1-902463-90-0
Lawrence the Lion gets a shock when the barber finds nits in his mane. Doctor Spot tells Lawrence's class all about nits.

Mike has Chicken-pox ISBN: 1-902463-38-2
Mike the Monkey comes out in spots and feels uncomfortably itchy. Doctor Spot prescribes a soothing lotion.

Rachel has Eczema ISBN: 1-902463-92-7
Rachel the Rhino is sore and itchy and can't sleep at night. Doctor Spot prescribes ointments and dressings which soon make her feel better.